Tuesday

Monday

Thursday

Satu

for Shelley
N.M.

for Annabel
A.A.

Published by
PEACHTREE PUBLISHERS, LTD.
494 Armour Circle NE
Atlanta, Georgia 30324

Text ©1995 by Nicola Moon
Illustrations ©1995 by Alex Ayliffe

First published by Orchard Books in Great Britain in 1995.

First United States edition by Peachtree Publishers, Ltd. in March, 1997.

Printed in Belgium

10 9 8 7 6 5 4 3 2

Library of Congress Cataloging-in-Publication Data
   Something special / Nicola Moon; illustrations by Alex Ayliffe.—lst ed.
     p. cm.
   Summary: Charlie can't find anything to take to school to show for "special" day, until he remembers that he does have a new baby sister.
   ISBN 1-56145-137-1
   [1. Show-and-tell presentations—Fiction. 2. Babies—Fiction. 3. Brothers and sisters—Fiction. 4. Schools—Fiction. 5. Blacks–England—Fiction.   I. Ayliffe, Alex, ill. II. Title.
   PZ7.M776So 1997
   [E]—dc20
                            96-24127
                               CIP
                               AC

Something Special

Nicola Moon

Illustrations by
Alex Ayliffe

PEACHTREE
ATLANTA

Friday was "special" day in Mrs. Brown's class. Everyone was allowed to bring in one of their favorite, special things to show the class.

"What can I take that's special?" asked Charlie one Friday morning. Mom was busy feeding Sally. "What about your teddy bear?" she said.

"Lots of people take their teddy bears," said Charlie.
"I want to take something different."
Sally started crying.
"Look in your bedroom," said Mom.

Charlie searched through his things.
There was Bessie, the old rag doll from
Africa that had belonged to his grandma.
But she didn't look very special with her
stuffing coming out.

There was the model boat he'd made
all by himself. But it fell apart as soon
as he tried to pick it up.

There was the beautiful chocolate
rabbit he'd saved from Easter.
But one ear had been bitten off.

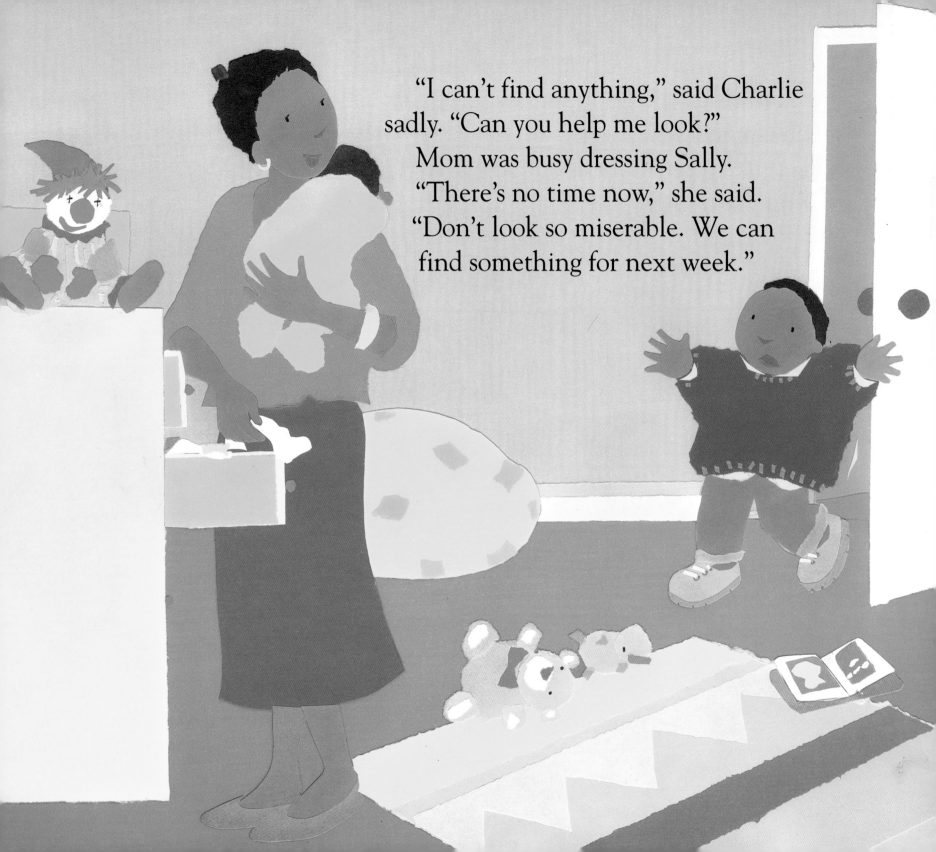

"I can't find anything," said Charlie sadly. "Can you help me look?" Mom was busy dressing Sally. "There's no time now," she said. "Don't look so miserable. We can find something for next week."

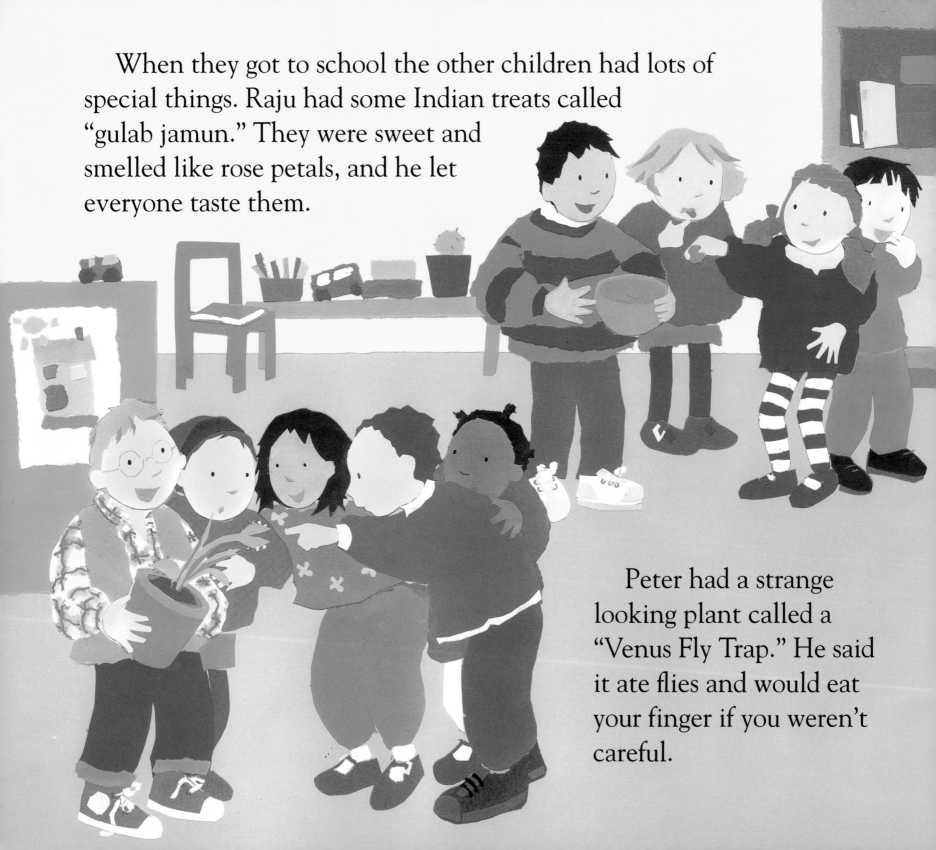

When they got to school the other children had lots of special things. Raju had some Indian treats called "gulab jamun." They were sweet and smelled like rose petals, and he let everyone taste them.

Peter had a strange looking plant called a "Venus Fly Trap." He said it ate flies and would eat your finger if you weren't careful.

Lu Mei had a beautiful kite. It was made of bright red paper and shaped like a dragon. She said it came from China.

Charlie's best friend Steven brought in his
pet hamster in a cage. Steven said its name was
Biscuit and Joanne said it looked like a rat.

And Daniel had a huge slimy worm
that he'd found on the way to school,
but Mrs. Brown made him put it outside.

Shireen had a beautiful sari that sparkled blue and gold. She put it on and Mrs. Brown said she looked like a princess.

But Charlie had nothing.
"Never mind," said Mrs. Brown. "You can bring something to show us next week."

"But I haven't got anything special," said Charlie on his way home. "Not special and different."

"What about your favorite book? Or Goldie the fish? Or your collection of postcards from Uncle Ali in Nigeria?"

Mom tried hard to think of something.

"No, I don't want to take those," said Charlie.

When they got home Mom had to feed Sally again.
And change her diaper. And wash her clothes.
And put her to bed.

Charlie felt cross. He turned the television on really loud. He stamped around and slammed the door.

"Ssh! You'll wake your sister," said Mom.

"I don't care!" said Charlie to himself.

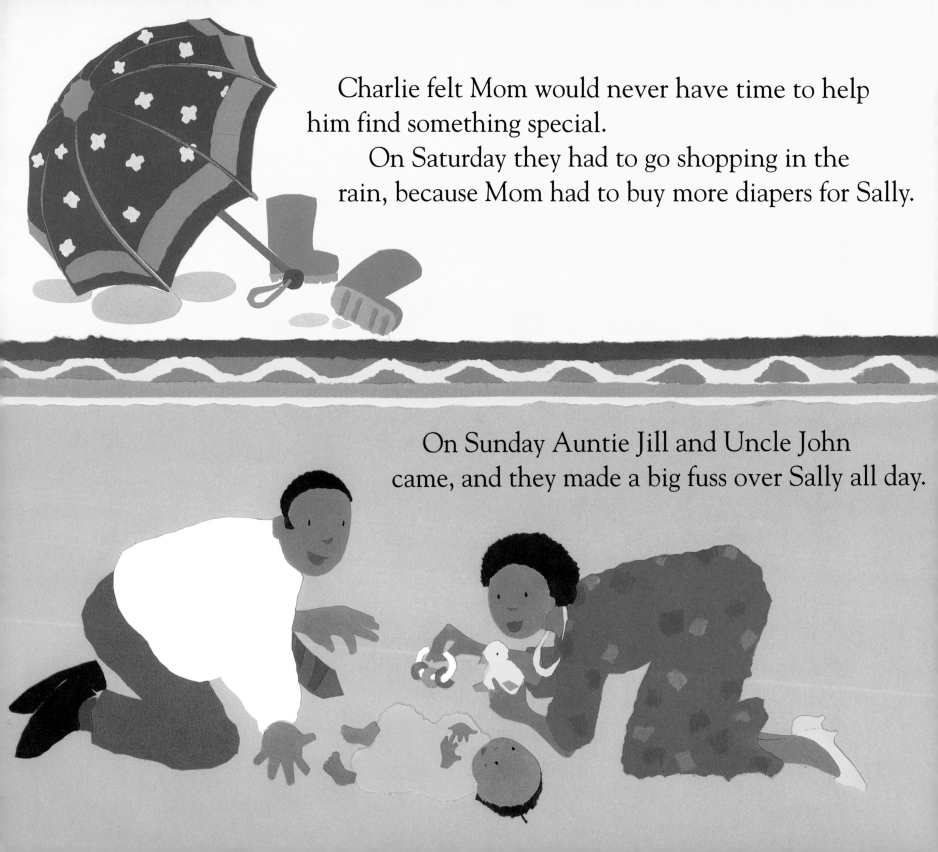

Charlie felt Mom would never have time to help
him find something special.
On Saturday they had to go shopping in the
rain, because Mom had to buy more diapers for Sally.

On Sunday Auntie Jill and Uncle John
came, and they made a big fuss over Sally all day.

On Monday they were late for school because Sally had cried all night and they slept late.

On Tuesday Charlie went to Steven's house for a snack. Steven had lots of special things. "You can borrow something if you like," he said.

"But it wouldn't be mine," said Charlie.

On Wednesday Charlie felt very cross. He still couldn't think of anything special to take to school. And Sally was crying again. Mom was busy making cookies in the kitchen.

"You go to her," she said.

"I don't want to." Charlie stamped his foot and started to cry. "All she does is cry all the time and I haven't got anything that's special, nothing at all."

Mom took Charlie onto her knee. "We'll find you something, you'll see. Now you go up and see Sally for me while I get the cookies finished. Then you can have some warm from the oven, just how you like them."

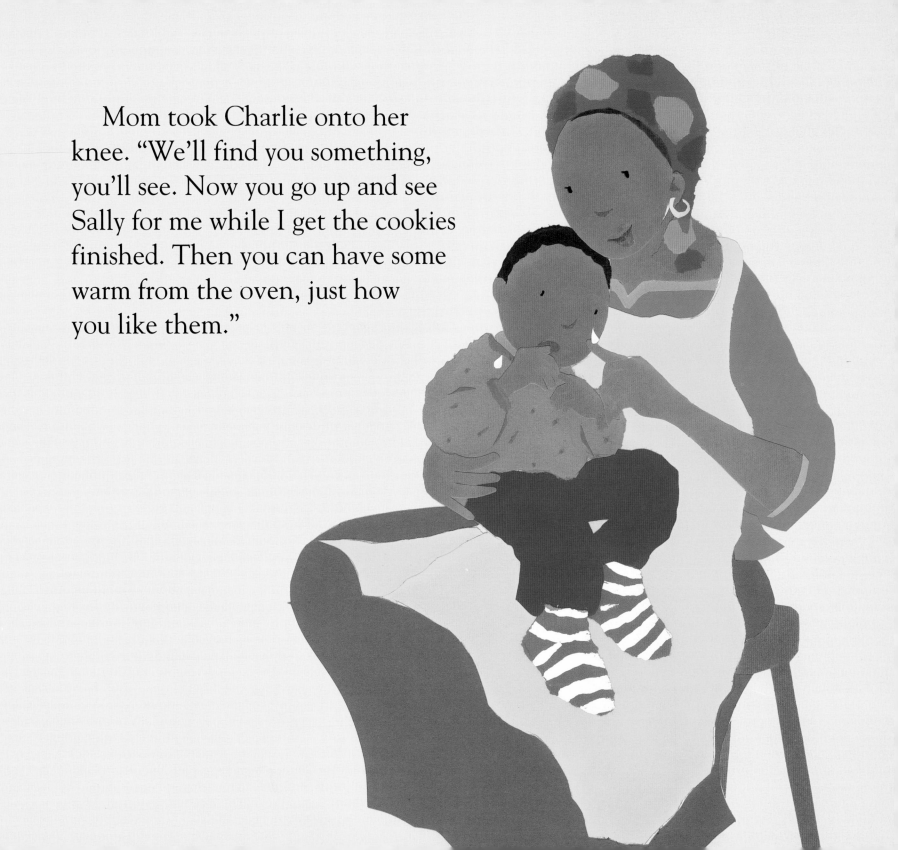

Charlie went slowly up the stairs and into Sally's room. He covered his ears and looked at his sister. Her face was all screwed up like an angry prune and she was kicking her legs wildly in the air.

"Stupid babies," he muttered. He picked up one of Sally's baby toys and started to play with it.

Sally stopped screaming. Charlie looked into the crib. Sally looked at Charlie with her big brown eyes. Charlie looked at Sally. Her hands were so tiny!

He reached out and touched her fingers. She grabbed
on to his finger so tightly he nearly cried out. But it felt nice.
He didn't know babies were so strong.

"Hello, Sally," he said. And then Sally
did something she'd never done before.
She smiled. A big beaming smile,
just for Charlie.

Later that evening Mom came to tuck Charlie into bed.
She held a wonderful carved wooden mask. "I've found
something for you to take to school," she said.
 "But I've already got something,"
said Charlie, and whispered in Mom's ear.

At school on Thursday Charlie was very excited.
"I'm bringing something really special tomorrow," he said.
"Is it a new toy?" asked Lu Mei.
"No," said Charlie.
"Is it your goldfish?" asked Steven.
"No," said Charlie.
"Is it something you can eat?" asked Daniel.
"No," said Charlie. "I'm not telling."

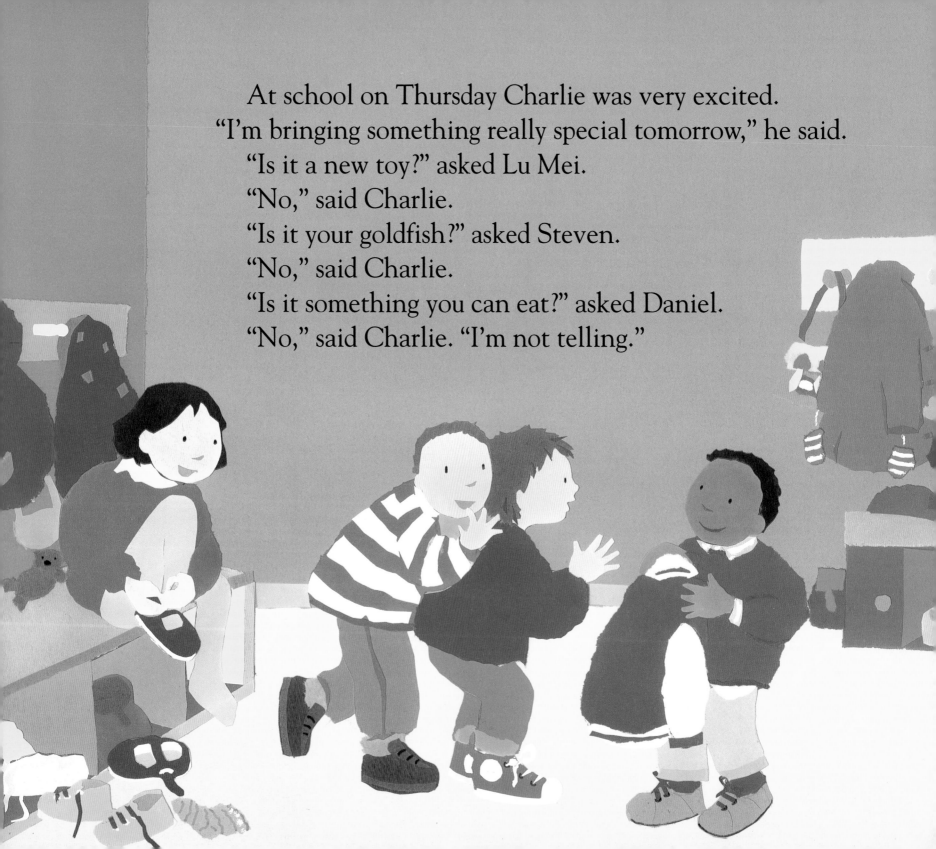

At last it was Friday. The other children were already waiting when Mom brought Charlie into the classroom.

"Charlie has something special to show us this morning," said Mrs. Brown.

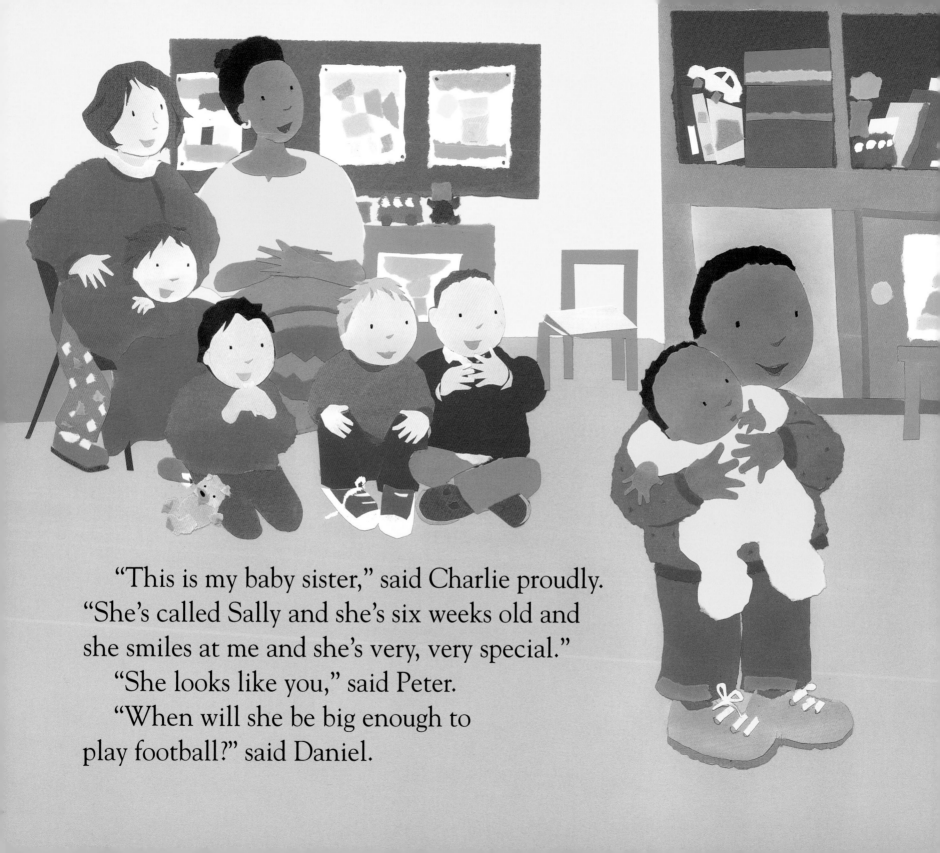

"This is my baby sister," said Charlie proudly. "She's called Sally and she's six weeks old and she smiles at me and she's very, very special."

"She looks like you," said Peter.

"When will she be big enough to play football?" said Daniel.

"You are lucky," said Joanne.
"I wish I had a baby sister," said Lu Mei.
"She isn't smiling at me," said Steven.
"She only smiles at me," said Charlie,
"because I'm her brother."

That night Charlie helped Mom bathe
Sally and put her to bed.
"Do you know what special day it will be
tomorrow?" asked Mom, when Sally was asleep.
"No," said Charlie.

"It's going to be big brother day," said Mom. "A special day for big brothers, because big brothers really are *something special.*"

Friday

Sunday

Wednesday

Saturday